Best In Show
by
Mike Peters

A TOM DOHERTY ASSOCIATES BOOK
NEW YORK

This is a work of fiction. All the characters and events portrayed in this book are fictitious, and any resemblance to real people or events is purely coincidental.

GRIMMY: BEST IN SHOW

A Tor Book
Published by Tom Doherty Associates, Inc.
49 West 24th Street
New York, N.Y. 10010

ISBN: 0-812-50712-6

First edition: May 1990

Printed in the United States of America

0 9 8 7 6 5 4 3 2 1

I REALLY SHOULDN'T HAVE EATEN HER FAVORITE SWEATER.
2/13
..AT LEAST NOT WHILE IT WAS STILL ON THE HANGER.

100
9-17

NEWS
2
26

GO ON... MAKE MY DAY...

WHAT PIRATES MUST DO EVERY MORNING...

OF COURSE NO ONE'S WAITING ON US, YOU IDIOT... YOU'RE BLENDING INTO THE BACKGROUND.

2-2

TAƎ
©1987 Tribune Media Services, Inc.
All Rights Reserved
12-26
CHAMELEONS AT LUNCH
YUCK... I SHOULD'VE HAD A V-8

YEP.. I'M DEFINITELY DIGGING TOO DEEP.

HOW DO I GET MYSELF IN-TO THESE THINGS?
6-16
MIKE PETERS
©1987 Tribune Media Services, Inc. All Rights Reserved
MIKE PETERS
3/31
©1987 Tribune Media Services, Inc. All Rights Reserved

.. AND NOW MY LOVELY ASSISTANT WILL ENTER THE COCOON ... NOTICE SHE HAS NO WINGS.
8-19

8/22

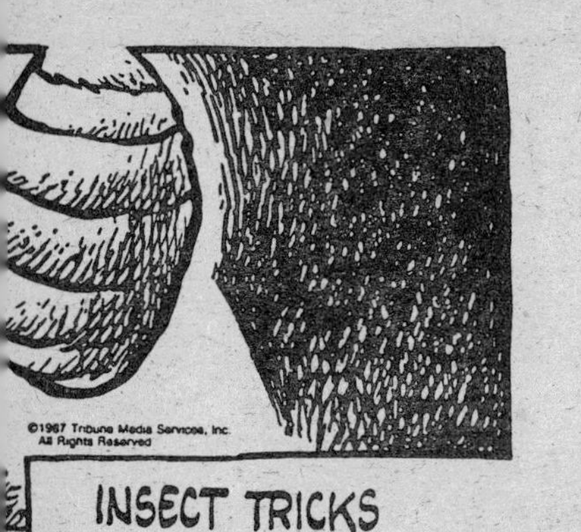
©1987 Tribune Media Services, Inc.
All Rights Reserved
INSECT TRICKS

TSK, TSK, AMY... YOU HAVEN'T BEEN USING THOSE LITTLE BIRDS TO CLEAN BETWEEN YOUR TEETH AGAIN...
©1987 Tribune Media Services, Inc.
All Rights Reserved

IS THE DOCTOR IN?

Tribune Media Services, Inc.
All Rights Reserved
DOG

I WISH THEY ALL COULD BE CALIFORNIA GULLS...
©1987 Tribune Media Services, Inc. All Rights Reserved

VET
10/20

LET'S DO LUNCH.

©1987 Tribune Media Services, Inc.
All Rights Reserved

©1987 Tribune Media Services, Inc.
All Rights Reserved

DON'T EVER TRY KISSING ME LIKE THAT AGAIN.

I JUST CAN'T SEEM TO COME OUT OF MY THIN CANDY SHELL.

Tribune Media Services, Inc.
All Rights Reserved
2-16

BETTER STOP GIVING HIM THOSE IRON PILLS...

LEE'S PRESS
ON SNAILS.
1-18

I DIDN'T KNOW SHE COULD THROW A FRISBEE THAT HARD.
Media Services, Inc.
Reserved

©1987 Tribune Media Services, Inc.
All Rights Reserved
10/12

I THINK HE WANTS TO GO FOR A RIDE.
8/21
MIKE PETERS
.. HELLO, MRS. CLEAVER, AND HOW'S THE BEAVER TODAY?
MIKE PETERS

1-2
the
NEWS

IF A MIME FALLS IN AN EMPTY FOREST DOES IT MAKE A SOUND?
HUEY, DEWEY AND LOUIE

RELAX... THE DOG STOPPED FOLLOWING US.
12-5
©1987 Tribune Media Services, Inc.
All Rights Reserved
OH OH... LOOKS LIKE THEY ONLY FEED YOU DOG FOOD, TOO...
©1987 Tribune Media Services, Inc.
All Rights Reserved

HMMM... A 37-LETTER WORD THAT SOUNDS QUITE ATROCIOUS... WHO COULD EVER FIGURE THIS ONE OUT?
CROSS-WORD

1/13

SURE, I'M GLAD THE KIDS ARE ALL GROWN... BUT, I MISS THE PITTER-PATTER OF LITTLE FEET.

GRIMM

I THINK IT'S TIME SHE CHANGED MY WATER BOWL.
©1987 Tribune Media Services, Inc. All Rights Reserved
IF ANYONE CALLS FROM THE NATURAL HISTORY MUSEUM, DON'T ANSWER IT.
3-24

10-5
I COULD'VE SWORN THERE WERE TWO POWDERED DONUTS HERE.
©1986 Tribune Media Services, Inc. All Rights Reserved
2-23
BA
2-14

SHALL WE LET HIM COME ALONG?

WHENEVER GEORGE COMES INTO A SINGLES BAR... HE ALWAYS SECRETLY REMOVES THE RING IN HIS NOSE.

THE NOSE IS TOO BIG. THE HANDS ARE WRONG. I DON'T LIKE THE COLOR.

HE SAYS HE WANTS A BOOK HE CAN SINK HIS TEETH INTO.
BRARIAN
WHISTLER'S MOTHER-IN-LAW

WIG

WHEN BALD EAGLES TURN 40

©1992 Tribune Media Services, Inc.
All Rights Reserved

HERE'S ONE... A THREE-YEAR-OLD COCKER SPANIEL WHO ANSWERS TO FLUFFY...

OUT-OF-WORK FLEAS

3-18

MRS. HOUDINI FIRST BECAME SUSPICIOUS WHEN SHE FOUND A STRANGE HARE ON HIS SHIRT.
OOOOW... RADICAL,
6-11

WAIT, DON'T TELL ME... YOU'RE THE POINTER SISTERS, RIGHT?
6/1
MIKE PETERS
I'VE FALLEN IN LOVE WITH A SIX-PIECE DINING ROOM SET.
4/3
MIKE PETERS

3-23
OK ATILLA, LET'S TRY IT AGAIN.

UGH...
UMPH
SUMO CHESS
TO BE HONEST, CARL...YOU'RE A GOOD DANE, BUT NOT A GREAT DANE.

4-15

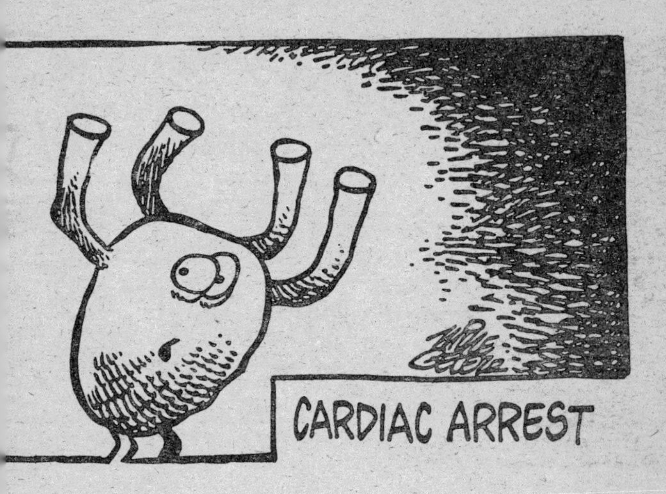

CARDIAC ARREST

2-12

FORTY-SEVEN,
FORTY-EIGHT,
FORTY-NINE,
FIFTY...
FIFTY-ONE...
12/8

SUDDENLY.. WITHOUT A WORD... MARGE AND ALDO REALIZED THE MAGIC HAD GONE OUT OF THEIR MARRIAGE.
5-4
MIKE PETERS
MR. POTATO PANCAKE

4-20

SEE... JUST AS I THOUGHT... BRASS KNUCKLES.

STRANGE... THIS ONE WAS CARRYING A BOX OF FROSTED FLAKES.
©1987 Tribune Media Services, Inc. All Rights Reserved

QUICK.. COME TO THE LAB... THE PROFESSOR CHANGED HIM-SELF IN TO A HUMAN FLY.
© 1985 Tribune Media Services, Inc.
All Rights Reserved

GESUNDHEIT.

LAB
10-9

SEX ED.
5-20

SAY... COME TO THINK OF IT... MINE HASN'T BROUGHT ME ANY LUCK EITHER...
A
B

SO, WE FINALLY MEET... I WAS HIRED BY AN OLD FRIEND OF YOURS, CAPTAIN AHAB...
OBSERVE THE CREW CUT... THE STEELY EYES... THE DISTINCTIVE ANCHOR TATTOO...
6-22

SHAMU THE KILLER WHALE

MARINE BIOLOGISTS

WELL, I'M FOLDING... I THINK HE'S GOT A GOOD HAND.

6-24

ME TOO.
HOW DO THEY KNOW? HOW DO THEY KNOW?
7/3
THE LONE RANGER AND HIS FAITHFUL INDIAN COMPANION

©1987 Tribune
All Rights Re

I THINK IT'S TIME YOU GOT RID OF THAT FISH TIE.
THAT'S RIGHT, MR. PATTERSON, MY NAME IS BAMBI... AND MAYBE YOU FORGOT WHAT HAPPENED TO MY MOTHER... BUT I DIDN'T.
5-26

DOG CATCHER
THIS DOGGY DOOR IS TOO SMALL...
PETS

US MAIL
IS THIS A GREAT COUNTRY OR WHAT?
1-28

Tribune Media Services, Inc.
All Rights Reserved
9-9
MAIL
STRANGE... I JUST SMASHED A LIGHTNING BUG, WEARING A LITTLE GREEN SWIMMING SUIT...

GRIMM... THE DOGGY DOOR IS DOWN THERE.

©1987 Tribune Media Services, Inc
All Rights Reserved
8/17

I TOLD YOU TO STOP BITING YOUR NAILS.

FETCH THE BONE AND I'LL TEACH YOU THE MEANING OF LIFE.

IS YOURS A BOXER?

SOCRATES AND PLUTO
8-5

NO.. HE'S IN-TO NINJA.

LIBRARIAN
11-24

OH, RELAX, HARVEY... IT LOOKS DEAD TO ME.
10 29

PIZZA
12-26

ANY SCRATCH-AND-SNIFF BOOKS?...
CLOSER.. CLOSER...

DID YOU ORDER A PIZZA WITH EVERYTHING?

6-3

WET
PAINT
6-8

WHY WAS I THE LAST TO KNOW THEY RAISED THE SPEED LIMIT?
©1987 Tribune Media Services, Inc.
All Rights Reserved

I THINK I WILL.

©1987 Tribune Media Services, Inc.
All Rights Reserved

GIVE... ME... A.. COLD... ONE..
10-6
©1987 Tribune Media Services, Inc.
All Rights Reserved

HAPPY HOUR OF THE LIVING DEAD

NO, NO, YOU IDIOT.. I SAID, JUGULAR... GO FOR A JUGULAR.
BRAIN

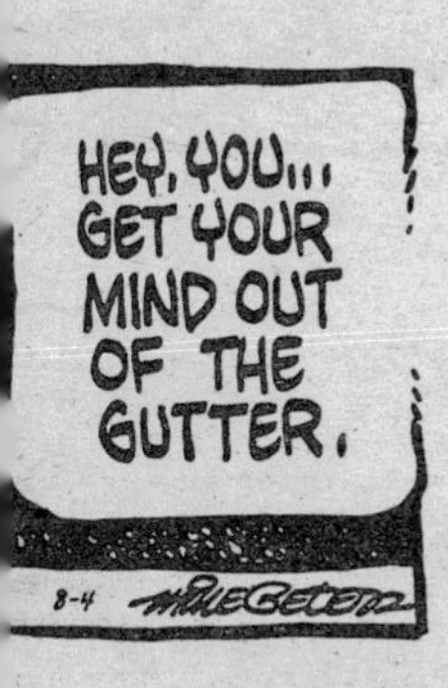
HEY, YOU... GET YOUR MIND OUT OF THE GUTTER.
8-4

1-16
I HATE GOLDEN RETRIEVERS.

SO CLOSE.
YET SO FAR
AWAY...

2-25

12/7

OH..DO YOU
WANT TO
GO OUT?

USA TODAY
USA TODAY

RALPH..ARE YOU GOING TO LET YOUR DAUGHTER GO OUT LIKE THAT ?...

I USE IT EVERY DAY...
© 1988 Tribune Media Services, Inc.
All Rights Reserved
2-3
MIKE PETERS

©1993 Tribune Media Services, Inc.
All Rights Reserved

SAND...I'VE ALWAYS LIKED SAND...I USED TO HAVE A SAND BOX ONCE... DID YOU EVER NOTICE ABOUT SAND, THAT...

NIGHT AFTER NIGHT, GOING THROUGH YOUR FAMILY HISTORY, I'M SICK OF YOU LOOKING FOR YOUR ROOTS,

RED CAPE... THEY...SAID... GO FOR ... THE....RED... CAPE.....
11/3

MAROONED WITH ANDY ROONEY
4-8

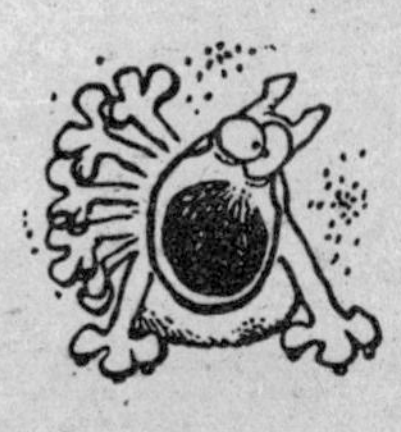

6-23
THE MAILMAN... CALL OFF THE MAILMAN.

BUS STOP
7/2

SHE HATES WHEN I DO THIS...

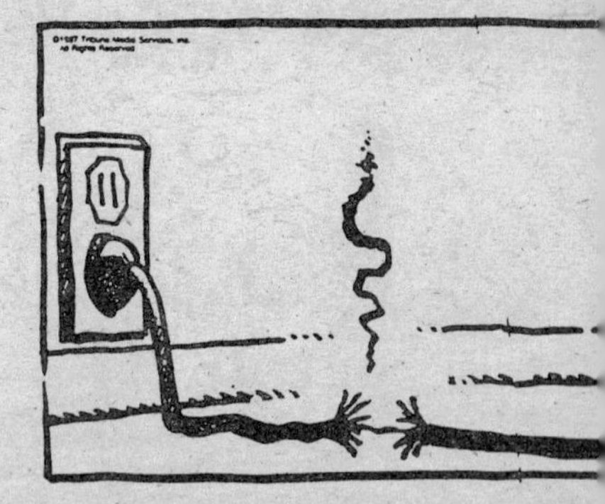
©1987 Tribune Media Services, Inc.
All Rights Reserved

WHO'S THE CLOWN WHO THREW THE DISCUS?....
7-22

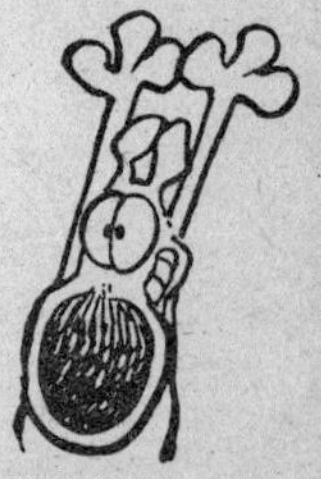

LESSON # 1... SNAKES DON'T CRAWL OUT OF ELECTRIC OUTLETS.
7-20

FLEA
MARKET
7-14
©1987 Tribune Media Services, Inc.
All Rights Reserved

OK, I'LL WAIT OUT HERE, GUYS... BUT DON'T TAKE TOO LONG.

HAVE YOU SEEN A DOCTOR ABOUT THIS?

THE WICKED QUEEN WENT THAT WAY...

SNOW WHITE AND THE MAGNIFICENT SEVEN
© 1988 Tribune Media Services, Inc.
All Rights Reserved

CAPTAIN... I THINK THIS IS THE DISNEY CHANNEL.
1-4

IS THAT CATCHING, OR WHAT?
1-10

9/18
GRIMM

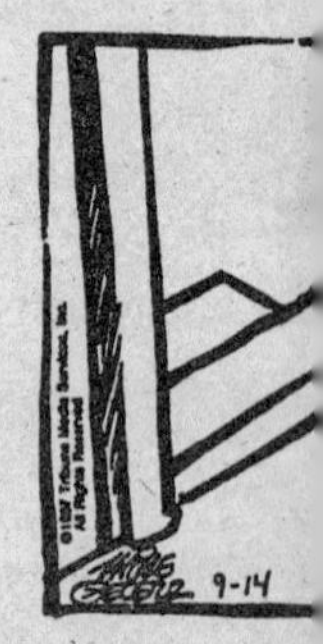
9-14

OH-OH.. LOOK OUT... WHEN THEY DO THAT THEY'RE ABOUT TO STRIKE.

OH, OH.... LEFTOVERS AGAIN.
©1987 Tribune Media Services, Inc. All Rights Reserved
CAREFUL, GRIMM, I JUST WAXED THE FLOOR.

UNFAIR

Tribune Media Services, Inc
All Rights Reserved
MIKE PETERS
11-19

©1987 Tribune Media Services, Inc.
All Rights Reserved
1-7
MIKE PETERS

WINNIE THE PUNK

DO YOU MIND ?.... AFTER ALL, THAT WAS MY AUNT HARRIET.

© 1988 Tribune Media Services, Inc.
All Rights Reserved

I HATE WHEN YOU START CURLING UP WITH A GOOD BOOK...
7/15

OH, LOOK... THE HENDERSONS HAD A BABY...
US MAIL

HELLO, MASTER..
3-30

TV
©1987 Tribune Media Services, Inc
All Rights Reserved

THE LAST EPISODE OF "I DREAM OF JEANNIE"

HI... WE'RE THE CREATURES FROM THE BLACK LAGOON... GOOD MORNING, AMERICA!

OH, OH... A SWISS ARMY ANT.
PSST.. HAVE YOU EVER THOUGHT OF PORCELANA?

RELAX... THE FIRST CAT SCAN IS ALWAYS A LITTLE SCARY.

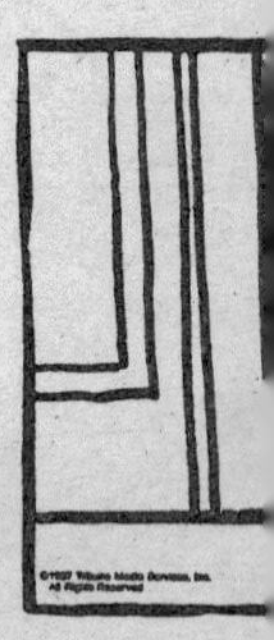

GEORGE.. IT'S ALL OVER BETWEEN US... YOU'RE HISTORY.

X-RAY

I THINK IT'S TIME TO CLEAN OUT MY BELLY BUTTON.
1-3

Tribune Media Services, Inc.
All Rights Reserved
12-27

R
4/21

GRIM
WHO UNPLUGGED MY ELECTRIC BLANKET?
THE FIRST ROBIN OF SPRING...
©1987 Tribune Media Services, Inc.
All Rights Reserved

©1987 Tribune Media Services, Inc
All Rights Reserved

10-8
©1987 Tribune Media Services, Inc.
All Rights Reserved

I KEEP SEEING A COVERED WAGON RUNNING THROUGH MY KITCHEN...
TAXI
OK, OK... I ADMIT IT... I'M A YELLOW CAB AND I'LL ALWAYS BE A YELLOW CAB.

12/8

CHOCOLATE! SO, YOU MELTED IN SOMEONE'S HANDS LAST NIGHT, DIDN'T YOU?
ALL I SAID WAS I WAS A VET...

IT'S YOUR BID.

1-30
ARK

YOU LOCKED THE DOGGY DOOR AGAIN.
10-7

© 1985 Tribune Media Services, Inc.
All Rights Reserved

STRIP POKER

OH, STOP COMPLAINING. DO YOU KNOW HOW MUCH WE'RE SAVING BY NOT GOING ON THIS CRUISE?

GATORADE 5¢

6-15

©1988 Tribune Media Services, Inc.
All Rights Reserved

PSST... 009. I THINK SOMEBODY SLIPPED YOU A MICKEY.

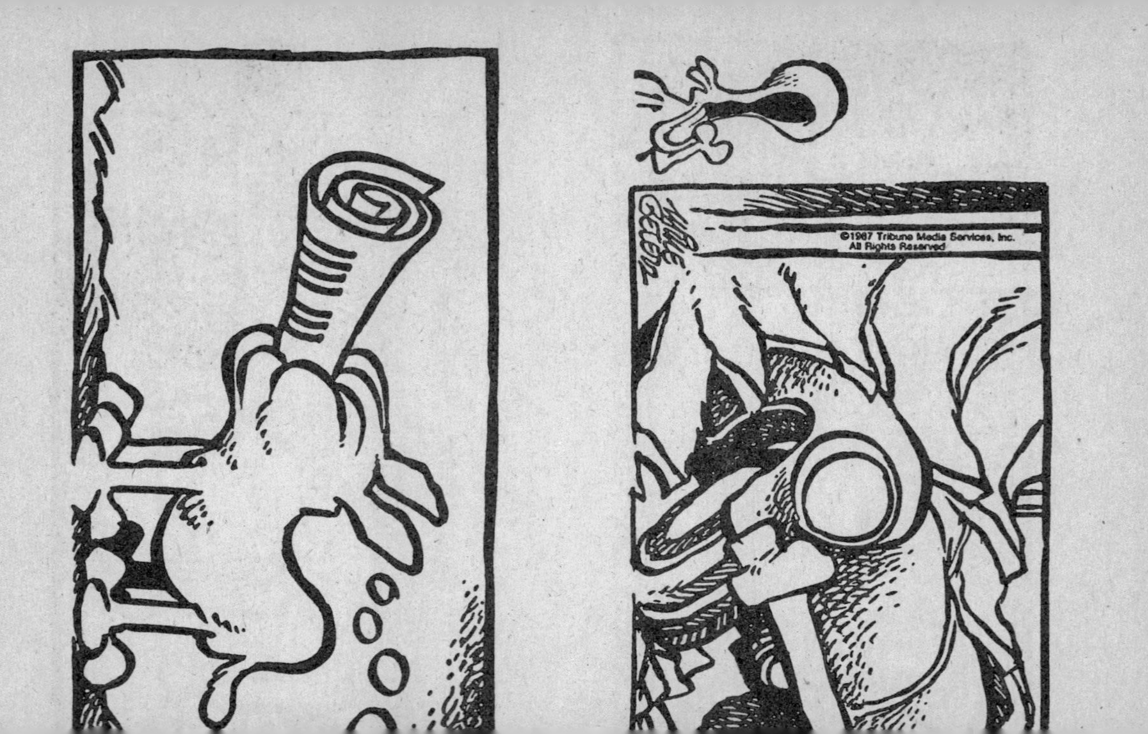
©1987 Tribune Media Services, Inc.
All Rights Reserved

IT FOLLOWED ME HOME, CAN I KEEP IT?

THAT PAPERBOY CAN SURE THROW...

CHAIN SAW OUT OF GAS, HUH? SURE...I'LL FILL IT FOR YOU...
HERB

OF COURSE I'M PUTTING HORSERADISH ON MY DOG FOOD... AFTER ALL, WHAT IS DOG FOOD?..IT'S HORSE...RIGHT?

HERB'S LAST SALE
9-8
TV
11-21
DOG COMMERCIALS

DON'T MOVE YOU DIRTY, LOUSY SLIMEBALL... CAN YOU SAY SLIMEBALL?
12-24

MY THREE
-IN-ONE
PROTECTIVE
COLLAR
RAN OUT.
12-10

MR.ROGERS NEIGHBORHOOD WATCH

NO,WAIT..YOU GOT
THE WRONG GUY...
I'M JUST THE
GRINCH WHO STOLE
GROUNDHOG DAY...

YOUR HONOR..THE PROSECUTION IS PUTTING WORDS IN MY CLIENT'S MOUTH.
THIS HORROR IS BROUGHT TO YOU BY THE LETTER H...
6-29
VET
I'D LIKE YOU TO SEE MY DOG.

7-13
NIGHTMARE ON
SESAME ST.
I'D LIKE
YOU TO
SEE MY
GOOSE.
11-27

COME ON, GRIMM.. TRY THIS FRISBEE JUST ONCE.
CHOMP
8-17
NEEDS SALT...

ISN'T THIS BEAUTIFUL?....
POEMS
© 1988 Tribune Media Services, Inc
All Rights Reserved
"I THINK THAT I SHALL NEVER SEE A POEM LOVELY AS A TREE..."
DITTO...
4-1

12-4

EBENEZER SCROOGE BEING VISITED BY THE SPIRIT OF ST. LOUIS.

HAVE A NICE DAY.
CONFUSED AND ALONE, HIAWATHA KNEW HE HAD FINALLY COME TO THE HAPPY HUNTING GROUND...

GRIMM.. I THINK IT'S TIME I TOOK YOU TO A DOG-TRAINING CLASS...
9-5
YOU'RE TOO LATE...
I ALREADY KNOW HOW TO BE A DOG.

It's GRIMMY
TM
America's Favorite Naughty Dog
Comes To Life In Brilliant Color.
The Highest Quality 100% Cotton T's,
And 50/50 Poly/ Cotton Blend Sweatshirts
TM & ©1990 Grimmy Inc.
All Rights Reserved
Licensed ByMGM/UA
Lin-Tex Marketing
Austin, Texas
GET YOUR SHIP TOGETHER...
SHIP
CRANK UP!
CRANK
BETTER
THE SURGEON GENERAL SAYS ALWAYS WEAR YOUR RUBBERS
RUBBER
IS IT OKAY TO LICK ON THE FIRST DATE?
LICK
SAFE SEX
SAFSEX
Life... YOU NEED NOT BE PRESENT TO WIN!
TOWIN
DECISI
See Other Side For Order Form

T-SHIRT & SWEATSHIRT ORDER FORM

Name ____________________

Address ____________________

City ____________ State ______ Zip ________

Home Phone ____________ Work Phone ____________

Charge My: ☐ VISA ☐ MasterCard ☐ Check Enclosed

Card Number ____________________ Exp. Date ________

Signature ____________________

Design	Qty. each Size	Price ea	Ext. Price
Rubber TE	S___ M___ L___ XL___	$12.95	
Rubber SW	M___ L___ XL___	$22.95	
Safsex TE	S___ M___ L___ XL___	$12.95	
Safsex SW	M___ L___ XL___	$22.95	
Better TE	S___ M___ L___ XL___	$12.95	
Better SW	M___ L___ XL___	$22.95	
Ship TE	S___ M___ L___ XL___	$12.95	
Ship SW	M___ L___ XL___	$22.95	
Lick TE	S___ M___ L___ XL___	$12.95	
Lick SW	M___ L___ XL___	$22.95	
Crank TE	S___ M___ L___ XL___	$12.95	
Crank SW	M___ L___ XL___	$22.95	
Towin TE	S___ M___ L___ XL___	$12.95	
Towin SW	M___ L___ XL___	$22.95	
Decisi TE	S___ M___ L___ XL___	$12.95	
Decisi SW	M___ L___ XL___	$22.95	
	Postage & Handling $2 x______ Items =		
	Texas Residents add 7.75% Sales Tax		
	Total		

TE= T-shirt SW= Sweatshirt

Mail To: Lin-Tex Marketing, Inc.
4930 S. Congress Ave.
Austin, TX 78745

Or Call: 1-800-847-5749
1-512-462-0056